For Otis with love
~ M. C. B.

For my sister-in-law, Vicky Greensit
~ T. M.

tiger tales
5 River Road, Suite 128, Wilton, CT 06897
Published in the United States 2016
Originally published in Great Britain 2016
by Little Tiger Press
Text copyright © 2016 M. Christina Butler
Illustrations copyright © 2016 Tina Macnaughton
ISBN-13: 978-1-68010-034-1
ISBN-10: 1-68010-034-3
Printed in China
LTP/1800/1440/0216
10 9 8 7 6 5 4 3 2 1

For more insight and activities, visit us at www.tigertalesbooks.com

One Noisy Night

by M. Christina Butler • Illustrated by Tina Macnaughton

tiger tales

Little Hedgehog and his friends were having breakfast.

"Did you hear the creaking and crashing last night?" asked Rabbit.

"I certainly did," said Badger.

"I didn't hear a thing!" said Little Hedgehog. "Was it the snow melting?"

"It was louder than that," said Fox. "I'm going to find out what's going on!"

That night, the noises
were louder than ever!

Creak!

Groan!

Crash!

Fox jumped up and crept outside.
As he tiptoed through the moonlit
trees, he saw a red hat bobbing
up and down near the river.
"Is that you, Little Hedgehog?" he cried.
But the hat disappeared, and
Fox went home even more
curious than before.

The next morning, Fox went to see Little Hedgehog.

"What were you doing in the woods last night?" Fox asked.

"I wasn't in the woods! I was home," replied Little Hedgehog.

"Oh," said Fox. "I was sure it was you! I must have been seeing things."

That night, Fox heard
the strange sounds
again. He tiptoed into the
woods and bumped into Badger
at the riverbank.
"Do you know what's making
those noises?" asked Fox.
"No," whispered Badger. "But wait!
Is that Little Hedgehog?"
"It is!" cried Fox. "Quick! Follow me!"

But as Fox ran one way, Badger turned the other way and they bumped into each other with a CRASH!

"You went the wrong way!"
cried Fox.
"I didn't," snapped Badger.
"Little Hedgehog was over there.
I'd know his red hat anywhere!"
"Humph. He's gone now,"
grumbled Fox. "We'll just have
to ask him tomorrow."

The next morning, the friends rushed over to
Little Hedgehog's house.

"Hello!" he beamed. "I was just putting out these sandbags
in case the river floods."

"We saw you down there last night!" said Badger.
"What were you doing?"

"But I haven't been near the river!" insisted Little Hedgehog.

"I'm *sure* it was him," mumbled Fox as they
walked home. "So why wouldn't he tell us?"

"Maybe he's planning a surprise," said Badger.
"It's all very strange."

That evening, Little Hedgehog couldn't stop thinking about the strange noises. "I wonder what they are," he said. "They have nothing to do with me! I'll have to stay awake and find out for myself."

But it was so warm by the fire, he soon fell fast asleep.

Suddenly, a huge CRASH! shook the house.
"Oh, my!" gasped Little Hedgehog, and he
ran outside.

Badger, Fox, and Rabbit were already
by the river.

"Look over there!" cried Fox.
"It's Little Hedgehog!"

"No, it isn't!" said a small voice
behind them. "I'm right here!"

Everyone spun around.
"If you're here," gulped
Rabbit, "who's that over there?"
"And there!" shouted Fox, pointing
to another red hat.
"Never mind that—look at the river!"
Little Hedgehog cried.
The water was swirling
higher and higher,
until . . .

. . . SWOOSH! The riverbank gave way and the water roared toward them.

"Get back!" yelled Little Hedgehog.

But Rabbit wasn't quick enough, and he was swept off his feet!

"Quick!" squeaked
Little Hedgehog. "Hold on to me."
    Rabbit clung tightly to Little Hedgehog
as Badger pulled them away from the swirling water.
    "You saved Rabbit!" Badger cheered.

But now the water was sweeping over the bank and down through the woods!

"Help! Our homes will be washed away!" yelled Fox.

"Look!" Rabbit called out.

Two beavers in red woolly hats were pushing a huge tree toward them.

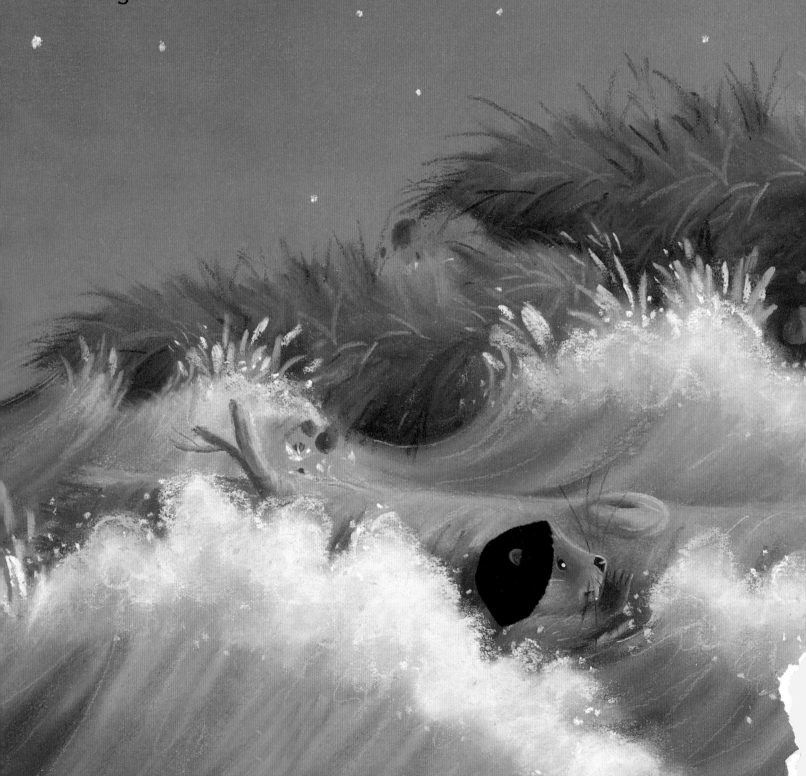

"They're trying to fix the bank and stop the flood!" cried Little Hedgehog. "Quick! Grab that tree!"

Together they guided the tree to the riverbank.

"Stand back!" called Little Hedgehog.

The tree settled on the riverbank, and the water swirled back down the river again.

"It worked!" Fox cried.

"You saved our homes from the flood," cheered Badger. "Great job, beavers! I think we all need a cup of hot chocolate to celebrate!"

"So the red hats we saw were the beavers' hats, not yours, Little Hedgehog!" grinned Badger.

"We were chopping down trees to make a dam in the river," they explained.

"And that's what the noises were!" laughed Fox.

"Thank you for rescuing me!" said Rabbit, smiling at Little Hedgehog.

"Hooray for Little Hedgehog and the beavers!" cried Badger.

And the friends all cheered for the heroes in red hats!